First published in English 2010 by order of the Tate Trustees
by Tate Publishing, a division of Tate Enterprises Ltd,
Millbank, London SW1P 4RG
www.tate.org.uk/publishing

First published in Portuguese as *Quando Eu Nasci*
© Planeta Tangerina, Isabel Minhós and Madalena Matoso 2007
English language edition © Tate 2010

A catalogue record for this book is available from the British Library
ISBN 978 1 85437 958 0

Distributed in the United States and Canada by Harry N. Abrams, Inc., New York
Library of Congress Control Number: 2010924849

Printed in Portugal by Printer Portuguesa

**Isabel Minhós Martins**
**Madalena Matoso**

# WHEN I WAS BORN

Tate Publishing

When I was born I had never seen anything.

Only the darkness
of my mother's tummy.

When I was born I had never seen the sun or a flower or a face.

I didn't know anybody
and nobody knew me.

When I was born
I didn't know what the sea was.
I didn't know that there were forests
and a world with mountains and beaches.

When I was born
I had never seen a bird
and I didn't know that some animals had feathers,
or that others had scales.

Or that others had hair, like my dog.

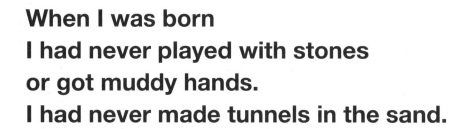

When I was born
I had never played with stones
or got muddy hands.
I had never made tunnels in the sand.

My hands had never touched anything
except each other.

When I was born
I did not know there was a sky
or that the sky could change
or that clouds were so beautiful.

When I was born everything was new.

Everything
was about to start.

My eyes were amazed
to discover
that everything is different.

Cherries are red.
Gardens are green.
The sea is blue.
My hat is yellow.
Little birds can be brown.
Clouds are white.
When the lights go out everything is black.

My mouth was amazed
to discover what it could do:
screaming,
laughing,
calling things by their names,
saying nice words and bad words,
kissing and sticking my tongue out,
tasting milk, soup, yogurt and fruit.

**Tasting everything
you can eat and drink.**

My nose was surprised too.

As soon as I was born
it was amazed by the strength
with which it pulled air into my body,
from then on it never stopped.
Every hour, every minute, every second
it brings me fresh new air and new smells.

These are the smells I love:
the smell of my grandmother's lap,
the smell of warm chicken soup,
the smell of paints in school,
the smell of my shampoo,
the smell of holidays
when summer arrives.

Inside my mother's tummy
I had already heard some voices,
even some music.

But I could not imagine
how the waves speak when
they come and go.
Or how, when the wind sings,
the trees sing too.

Or how nice it is when someone
whispers in your ear.
Or how loud it can be
when something falls.

PLIP

Or how a leaf falling
just goes: plip!

THUMP

When I was born my hands wondered:

What is this? Who are you?

And ever since then they have never stopped: always discovering, always learning, always opening and shutting things.

With them I have already found out
that some things are soft and that others are hard,
that some things are hot and others are cold,
and that some things
have other things inside them.

And that inside
those things
there are other things.
And inside those
things, there are
even more things...

With my hands
I can reach nearly everything.
But if I can't,
I stand on tiptoe.
When I was born my feet
didn't know how to walk.
But now they take me everywhere.

They let me run

And dance

And jump up and down on my bed.

When I was born I didn't know anything.
Now I know
that there is a whole world to discover:

millions and millions of things
my hands haven't yet reached;
millions and millions of lands
my feet haven't yet taken me to.

And new smells and sounds and tastes.

But one thing is certain.
Each day
I discover something new.

And that is the most
wonderful thing of all!